Fuzzy Chums

Totally Spotless

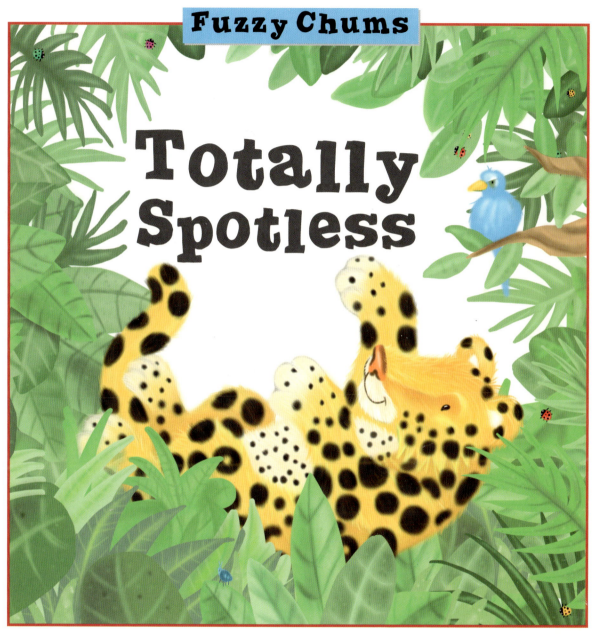

templar publishing

It was a hot day in the jungle.
Bobby Spots lay lazily in the sun.

"I am bored to the bottom of my spots!"
he said as he licked his spotted coat.

"What?" asked Monkey Marky,
swinging by on a branch.
"This jungle is filled with fun!" he exclaimed,
tapping Bobby on the nose.
"Tag! Catch me if you can!"

Monkey Marky raced off,
swinging from vine to vine.
Trying to catch him,
Bobby Spots grabbed a creeper.

"YE-OW!"

Bobby hadn't grabbed a thick vine
but Cobra's tail by mistake!

"Sorry," called Bobby as he leaped up into
a tree after Monkey Marky.

"That leopard is getting too big for his spots," muttered Cobra.

"Ha ha ha!"
chuckled Monkey Marky,
hanging from a branch.
"You confused Cobra
with a creeper!"

Bobby reached out a paw to catch
the cheeky monkey when there was a
horrible creaking sound and then a
CRACK!

Patiently fishing in a nearby pond,
Crane's beady eye was on
a delicious-looking fish, when –
SPLASH!

Bobby landed in the water with a yelp.
The delicious fish darted away.

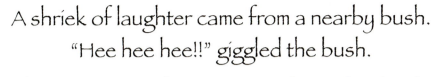

A shriek of laughter came from a nearby bush.
"Hee hee hee!!" giggled the bush.

There was something strange about that bush.
And it had a tail... Monkey Marky's tail!
Bobby Spots jumped after him.

Monkey Marky swung away, singing,
"Ha ha ha! Hee hee hee!
As hard as you try, you'll never catch me!"

Suddenly, there was a loud

"TOOT!"

Monkey Marky found himself
swinging from Elephant's trunk!

Bobby was just a whisker away from catching his friend, when –
"HARUMPH!"

he landed on Rhinoceros's back!

Without stopping to apologise,
the pair raced off.

"Watch me!" called Monkey Marky.
He picked a banana, peeled it carefully
and crammed it whole into his mouth.

"Ha ha ha! Hee hee h— urgh!"

A piece caught in his throat and he coughed.
Staggering backwards, he slipped on the
banana skin and fell on top of Tiger!
"GRRROAR!" roared Tiger.

"WAH!" screamed startled Antelope,
who had been grazing nearby.

Hearing the uproar, Cobra, Crane, Elephant
and Rhinoceros came over to see what the matter was.

"That monkey is getting much too mischievous," said Tiger.

"And that leopard is getting too big for his spots," said Antelope.

"I have an idea," said Cobra, "gather around."

"Would you two like to play a game?" Cobra asked the naughty pair a little later. "It's called Stuck in the Mud."

"Oh yes!" answered Bobby Spots and Monkey Marky.

"First you must both stand at the very edge of the swamp," said Cobra. "Follow me."

"Coming to get you!" shouted Rhinoceros, surprising the pair so much that they fell into the muddy swamp.

"Help!" shouted Monkey Marky.

"My spots are disappearing!" cried Bobby. "We don't like this game at all!"

"Now do you see that some games aren't fun for everyone?" asked Rhinoceros.

"Yes we do," said Bobby Spots.

"And we are sorry," added Monkey Marky.

"Well alright then," said Rhinoceros, and he waded in to rescue them both.

Bobby Spots licked his muddy fur.
"My spots!" he sobbed, "I've lost them forever!"

"Nonsense!" said Elephant and with a
"TOOT!" he hosed Bobby down
until his coat glistened gold and black.

"There Bobby, now you're totally spotless!"
said Monkey Marky, and everybody laughed.